GILLES
TIBO
PIKOLO'S
NIGHT VOYAGE

Text by Pierre Filion, based on an original idea by Tibo

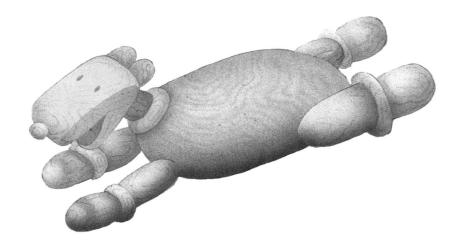

Annick Press

Annick Press gratefully acknowledges the support of the Canada
Council and the Ontario Arts Council.

Canadian Cataloguing in Publication Data
   Filion, Pierre, 1951-
      [Pikolo : l'arbe aux mille trésors. English]

   Issued in French under title: Pikolo : l'arbe aux mille trésors

   ISBN 1-55037-365-X (lib. bdg.)
   ISBN 1-55037-364-1 (pbk.)

   PS8561.I53p513 1994   jC843'.54   C93-095294-4
   PZ23.F5Pi 1994

Distributed in Canada by: Published in the U.S.A. by Annick Press (U.S.) Ltd.
Firefly Books Ltd.   Distributed in the U.S.A. by:
250 Sparks Ave.   Firefly Books (U.S) Inc.
Willowdale, ON M2H 2S4   P.O. Box 1338
                                   Ellicott Station
                                   Buffalo, NY 14205

Printed on acid-free paper.

Printed and bound in Canada by
D.W. Friesen & Sons, Altona, Manitoba.

To our Aunt Marthe

Uncle Roger came to visit Pikolo from his home deep in the forest. He brought a large, heavy gift.

As Pikolo eagerly tore open the package, his uncle explained, "When my father was a young boy, he planted a small tree, a sapling from a magnificent Treasure Tree at the end of the earth. No one has been able to find the Treasure Tree since then!

"That sapling grew to be the oldest tree in the forest. But one day it was struck by lightning. I took the broken trunk to the sawmill and had it made into lumber. Then I brought home the best boards and made this engine out of them. This is a special train, Pikolo. It has taken me to faraway, magical places. I want to give my train to you. Maybe you'll be the one to find the Treasure Tree."

All day long Pikolo played with his new engine. He travelled all around the house. But the engine did not take him anywhere magical.

That night, Pikolo crawled into bed, but he was too excited to sleep. With his engineer's cap on his head, he lay awake, admiring his wonderful train.

"That engine could use some cleaning," thought Pikolo, "so that it will be ready for tomorrow." He got out of bed, polished the headlights, and checked the wheels. Finally, he climbed aboard to test the motor.

"VROOM, VROOM," he cried.

VROOM, VROOM, VROOM, the engine roared back. The wheels screeched, stars flew out of the smokestack and suddenly Pikolo had lost control of his engine.

"Help! What is happening? I wish Uncle Roger was here!" The train started going faster and faster – straight into Pikolo's closet.

CHUG, CHUG, CHUG – Pikolo tried with all his might to turn the train around, but it was heading for the darkest corner of his closet.

"Whoa! I am going to crash," shouted Pikolo into the darkness.

But there was no crash. The train shot forward as the headlights burned a path in the dark. To his amazement, Pikolo could see train tracks leading into the starry night.

CHOO, CHOO, CHOO. Soon Pikolo saw that the sky was filled with trains driven by other children. "Hey, where are we going?" he yelled.

Then he heard: "GO, little train, GO, GO, GO.
We'll ride to the edge of the earth.
There we'll find the Treasure Tree,
The tree with a thousand treasures.
It's waiting for you and me."

Pikolo was so busy watching everything that he was surprised when the trains arrived at a station. It was built entirely out of trees. Some were so tall Pikolo thought they must surely touch the sky. This was Wood City, the strangest place he had ever seen. Everything – and everyone – was made of wood.

As his train rolled past the station, Pikolo reached out and grabbed a piece of paper.

"Perfect! It's a map! A map that will lead me to the Treasure Tree!" Clutching the map tightly, Pikolo explored Wood City, making friends on his way.

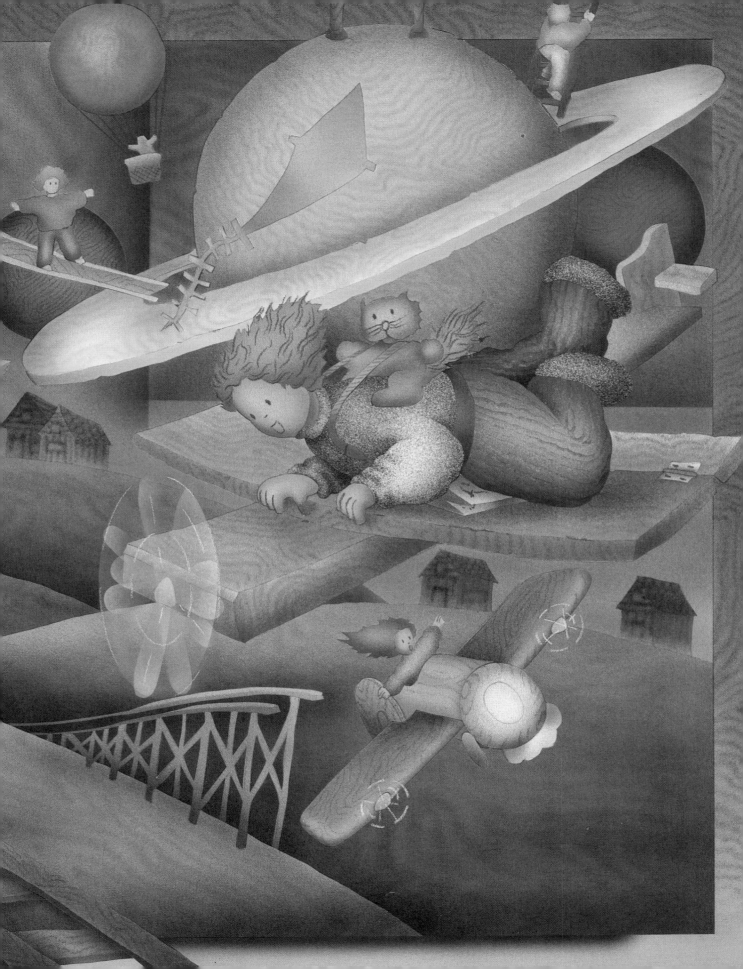

Pikolo played like he never had before. But all of a sudden, just as he got to the edge of Wood City, Pikolo stopped. Right in front of him was a huge maze.

"Help, I'm lost. How am I going to find my way through that?" he wondered. Then he remembered the map! Pikolo pulled it out and followed the directions.

VROOM, VROOM, VROOM. Pikolo put his engine on full speed. He had to hurry, nighttime was coming to an end and he still had to find his treasure.

As Pikolo quickly left the maze behind him, he heard the faint cry of children, "Hurry, hurry, time's running out." But suddenly, VROOM, CLUNK, CLUNK. What a terrible break! The engine slowed, quieted – and then stopped.

Pikolo did the only thing he could think of. He got off and pushed his train.
Far off in the distance he could see a merry-go-round. Then, finally, there at
the edge of the earth he saw an incredible tree – the Treasure Tree.

Pikolo drew closer and saw a ladder. He climbed up two steps at a time and reached for his special treasure chest.

Inside was a little sapling. Its flowers glowed like lights.

"Wow, I can't wait to show this to Uncle Roger." Pikolo smiled, so happy that he'd completed his quest. He knew exactly what he would do with his treasure.

Suddenly the wind began to blow fiercely. Pikolo remembered he was at the edge of the earth, his train had broken down, and it was almost sunrise. "How will I ever get home?" he wondered aloud.

Looking around, he came up with an idea. Pikolo hitched his broken-down engine to one of the merry-go-round horses, and climbed aboard.

"GIDDY-UP, GIDDY-UP," he called, as they headed towards home. "Oh, please hurry, beautiful horse. The night is almost over. GIDDY-UP."

And just before the first rays of the sun peeked out, Pikolo burst through the closet and into his bedroom.

Pikolo tumbled into bed, exhausted and happy. In the distance, he heard the rumbling of a train and the galloping of a horse. He snuggled under the covers and smiled. Tomorrow he would take his Treasure Tree sapling to Uncle Roger. Pikolo closed his eyes and dreamed about how they would plant the tree, together, deep in the forest...